John MacLush

Pious Jemima; a doleful Tale. With 180 illus

John MacLush

Pious Jemima; a doleful Tale. With 180 illus

ISBN/EAN: 9783337024758

Printed in Europe, USA, Canada, Australia, Japan

Cover: Foto ©Andreas Hilbeck / pixelio.de

More available books at **www.hansebooks.com**

Pious Jemima:

A Doleful Tale.

With 180 Illustrations.

EDINBURGH:
WILLIAM P. NIMMO.
1872.

EDINBURGH:
PRINTED BY M'FARLANE AND ERSKINE
(*Late Schenck & M'Farlane*),
ST JAMES'S SQUARE.

DEDICATION.

DEAR PUBLIC,

      This book suits the season,
For it is without rhyme or reason;
'Twas written when the black curator
Sat not behind the grim translator,
And is, except this dedication,
Naught but a very free translation,
Done from the German of Herr Busch
In th' English tongue by John MacLush.
I'm sure I'd no need to explain,
For to us, natives, 'tis quite plain,
Whate'er our faults in Britain be,
We ne'er a poor "Jemima" see,
And that we seldom moist our throttle,
With the contents of a black bottle:
Such things in foreign parts are seen,
Not here—therefore, long live the Queen!

CHAPTER I.

LIKE the wind in poplar grove,
Sounds the pious poet's ditty,
When he looks on vicious joys
In the big, enormous city.

Oh ! the papers are immoral !
For quite early in the day
They let all the townfolks know
The sinful doings of the gay.

Offenbach rules now the stage,
Of balls and concerts there are many.
Oh ! how joyful beat the hearts
Of Jeanie, Mary, and of Annie !

Scarcely has the cup been emptied,
They adorn the outward man,
And they crowd on street and boulevard,
Simply " pour passer le temps."

How they bow ! how they are staring !
Here are elegant mounseers ;

There the ladies with their sweetly
Heavenward tow'ring back-panniers.

With crooked nose and crooked hose,
The Jew, with crooked capriole,
Wriggles upward on th' Exchange, but
Without heart and without soul.

I won't mention all the places,
Where the wicked nightly go,   .
Where, amongst the lib'ral party,
They attack Pio Nono.

I won't mention e'en the concerts,
Where the connoisseurs delighted,
Look with piercing op'ra glass
To see if any soul is blighted;

Where, with soft and swelling bosom,
Ladies warmly crowd together;
Where the muses sing in chorus,
And the sage is in high feather.

I won't mention the theatre,
How, when it gets very late,
The fair mother and old father,
Arm in arm, walk home in state.

Though the young increase in number,
Th' old think nothing of their kind;
And when children grow up sinners,
Pa and ma say, " Never mind."

"Come, Jemima," says the honest
Guardian ; "come, my little fair ;
Come with me into the country,
Gentle sheep and lambs are there.

"There is uncle, there is aunty,
Virtue, and no money spent.
There are all thy 'parients,' darling ;"

So of course Jemima went.

CHAPTER II.

"Jemima!" said old uncle Jimmie,
"As man and Christian, 'tis my care
To tell you, what I'd often wish'd to,
Of all things evil do beware.
'Tis pleasant while the pleasures last,
But 't causes grief when they are past."

"Indeed, they're doomed!" said gentle auntie,
"These wicked! I've known many such!
Therefore a child should wisely learn
To honour all old people much!
For, though they once were rather loose,
They now, thank Heaven, are virtuōūs!

Now, good night; it is late already,
Jemima, dear, pray, and be steady!"

Jemima leaves the room. She sees
On uncle's bed his night chemise.

So quickly with her needle goes,
And neck and arms together sews.

Then in a trice pops into bed,
And pulls the blankets o'er her head.

Soon the old uncle does appear,
And seems a-gaping rather queer.

A final pinch of snuff tastes best
Before our uncle goes to rest,

And acting as a " cannie mon,"
He tries to put his night-shirt on.

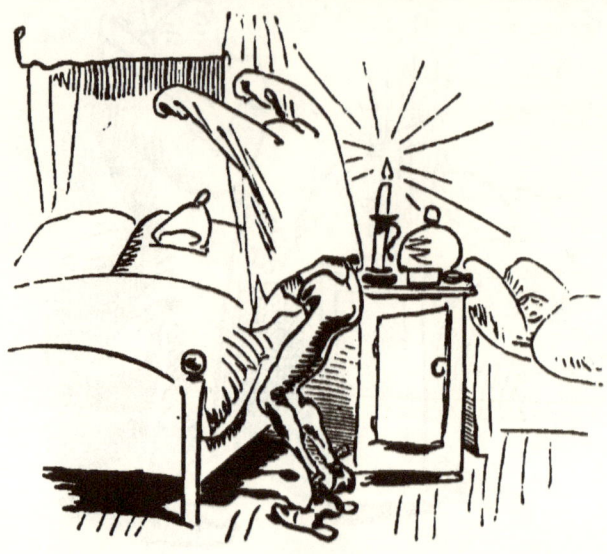

But, though he tries with might and main,
Yet all his efforts are in vain.

" By Jove ! will wonders never cease ! "
Says uncle, struggling with chemise.

He's working hard with main and might,
Behold ! Och hone ! down goes the light !

His wrath increases more and more,
Snuff-box and watch fall on the floor.

His wrath in actions does explode—
Slap bang ! there goes the night-commode.

At last the aunt comes on the scene,
But uncle feels now " all serene."

"O sinful, wicked, naughty puss!
Sleep on and snore, you little cuss!"

Jemima thinks, it is quite plain,
"I'll never do the like again!"

CHAPTER III.

Jemima is now quite grown up,

And does no longer look a fright.
" I say, my pet, you know the news—
Our cousin Frank arrived last night."
So spoke dear auntie, about eight,
While she was making coffee ready.
" Therefore, you're on your best behaviour,
And in your manners must be steady.
And don't you stoop too much at table,
And do not stare about you so ;
And let me recommend you, dear,
The green dress, that's cut out so low—
That dress you don't put on, I say,
But any other, yes, you may."

"What," thinks Jemima, "still asleep!"
And through the keyhole takes a peep.

Frank, tired, lies in deep repose,
And nothing but the bed-clothes shows.

"Ah ! ha !" he gapes, and tries to say
" It's time I should get up to-day.

And that without circumlocution,
I should perform my morn ablution.

For, *primo :* I much like the splashing.

Secundo : It is quite refreshing.

And *tertio :* One feels very dusty.

Quarto : Sans water one gets crusty.

Quinto : It beautifies the face,

And is good for the human race !

A traveller feels another man
When a clean shirt he put on can.

And really it is quite a blessing
When he at last can finish dressing,

And reap i' the end with great success

The harvest of his cleanliness."

Now cousin Frank his pipe has lit,
Jemima quickly tries to flit.

Zing Boum ! How woeful is her lot,
She stumbles o'er the wat'ring pot,

And falls upon the servant " gal,"
Who does not seem to like it well.

Jemima and the "gal" roll down
On coffee-bearing auntie's crown.

And when this hurly-burly's done,
Uncle's coffee is all gone.

CHAPTER IV.

FRANK was belov'd by every one
As learned, scholarly, and witty,
And in the middle of the night,
He composed the following ditty:

> Once upon a time,
> I walked through the wood,
> There a many-colour'd bird
> Sang and hoopdendo'ed.
> What the little birdie sang
> I feel well enough.
> Love was the theme; for the rest
> I don't care a snuff.

He gives this to Jemima, who
Liked and prais'd it very much,

And Frank was really very pleasant
For different reasons, many such.
If a nail has to be driven in,
Frank for the hammer goes and looks ;
If they go to the dark cellar,
Frank very quickly leaves his books.
For greens if they look anywhere,
In field or garden, Frank is there !

Oft 'tis troublesome to pluck
French beans that grow so very high.

Jemima cannot fall ; a hand
Holds firm the ladder—Frank is nigh !

And when above she's done and finish'd,

Frank assists her here below.

In short, whatever may turn up
Frank is in helping never slow.

And for these reasons, and therefore,
He has a lot of fun, galore !

Look ! yonder hops about the green
A froggie, caught as soon as seen !

And without any more ado,
Frank pops 't in uncle's snuff-box too.

c

A pinch of snuff dear uncle takes,
But lo ! how the box moves and shakes !

Oh ! dear ! the froggie upward springs—
To uncle Jimmie's nose it clings.

Splish ! splash ! it jumps right in the cup,
And of the coffee takes a sup.

Now 't hops into the muffin-plate,
And finds 'tis in an awkward strait.

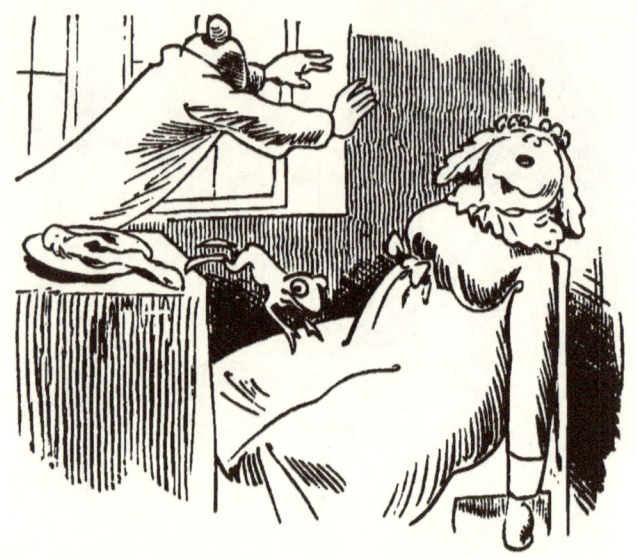

Och hone! what terror! what mishap!
The froggie leaps in auntie's lap.

Dear uncle Jim the bell-pull tries,
And "Jeanie! Jeanie! help!" he cries.

And Jeanie with courageous hand
Removes the monster, " à l'instant."

Whilst uncle wat'ry streams dispenses,
Dear aunt recovers quite her senses.

Oh! great fun 'twas for young Jemima,
The trick that cousin Frank had played,
But what she did not like at all

Was when he with the servants stay'd.
But every youth plays now and then,
Down in the kitchen many a prank,
And mankind on the whole is sinful!
Jemima prays for her dear Frank!

But there was one who bore a grudge—
Our uncle Jimmie, so prophetic,
He ne'er forgot the trick with froggie,
And felt then really quite splenetic.
He was, of course, so very glad,
When all the holidays were spent,
And Frank, with terror in his heart,
Back to the gymnasium went.

CHAPTER V.

"And even if uncle should get angry,
I do not care a little bit!"

Such were Jemima's inward thoughts
When she to her dear cousin writ :

" My dearest Frank ! I'm sure you know
That I am yours, and wholly so.

How very pleasant was that time,
Our hearts in unison did chime.

When in the bean-stalks Jack and Gill,
Of hearty kisses had their fill.

I tell no tales, and say not what——
Good heavens !   If auntie knew of that !

Alas !   Here in this poor countrie
There is no fun, no lightsome spree.

I'm glad to say Jim is not clever.

And auntie fidgets just as ever.
My dearest Frank, try to come, please,
For both are terrible devotees.
Do come, for nothing then amiss is.
Jemima sends a thousand kisses."

" I'll seal the letter now "—but, lo !

Uncle in thundering voice cries, " No ! "

And poor Jemima's face discloses,
The waxiest of ladies' noses.

CHAPTER VI.

In the bedroom dark and dreary,
Sleeps the uncle with his dearie.

Armed with line, and hook also,
Jemima draws near on tiptoe.

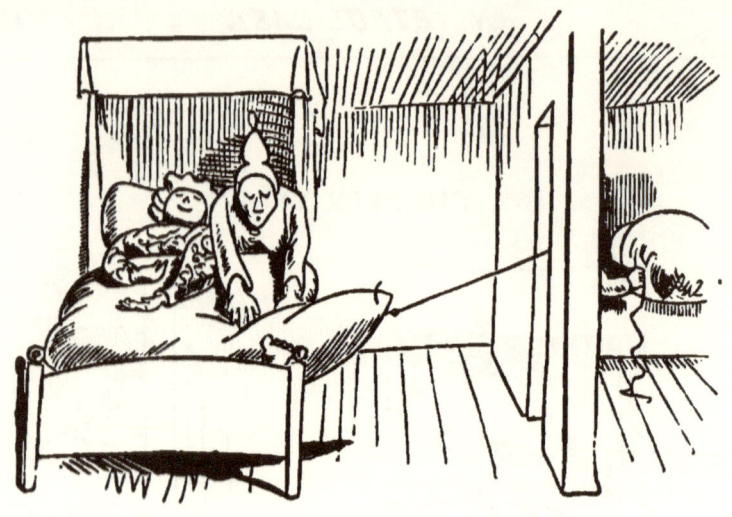

A pull! the top-bed flies away.
Uncle Jim shows great dismay.

A pull! and auntie, without clothes,
Feels the cold air on her toes.

"Jim," she shouts; "leave off, I pray.
Cease your funny tricks, I say."

Amidst mumbling and grumbling,
Each on their own side lie tumbling. .

Bang! The upper bed is off!
By the powers! that's quite enough.

Down comes now the bunch of keys.
Uncle out of bed he flees.

"But oh! oh! what pains me so?
I've a hook in my big toe!"

More and more pulls our Jemima.
Uncle shouts, "My foot is high, ma!"

D

Jemimā holds fast the door;
There's something for her in store.

By and by 'tis tranquil here,
And in silence sleep our dear.

But in the morning uncle Jimmie,
In hollow voice, yet calm and slow,
Made known what was before arranged,
And said, "Jemima, you must go."

But she replied, "Forgive me now.
I'll ne'er do it again, I vow."

"Too late! and without more ado,
Farewell! and take your trappings too."

CHAPTER VII.

It is always wise and good,
That any young lady should
Well select and choose a man,
Who will marry if he can.
Primo, it's the custom so,
Girls wish't, that's *secundo*—
Tertio, they want a friend,
Many hours with whom they spend.
Several jolly things, we know,
Don't suit Poll, but partner Joe.
For the lasses, fast or slow,
Ne'er alone to taverns go.

And e'en if propose they might,
Where can they find Mr Wright?
Lonely hours are often spent,
When they crave amusĕment.

Two canaries in a cage,
Are with our dear girl the rage.

One of the darlings was called Nip,
Th' other's name was only Pip.
Food from Jemima's hand they took :

But the kitten's name was "Suke."

Master Tom i' the house came running,
He was clever, bold and cunning.

And these two at once agree.
Quietly, but speedily,

They twist now, with murd'rous lust,
Nip's and Pip's neck off "at first."

Then they jump so warily,
On the table, full of glee ;
Sukie, with the velvet paws,
Gently the sweet biscuit claws.

Master Tom, so it would seem,
Appears to delight in cream.

Jemima, who had been upstairs
To write a letter, unawares
Enters the room, astonished stands,
With wax and paper in her hands.

Sukie hastily cuts away,
But poor Tom, alas, must stay.

In vain Tommie tries to lug,
His head sticks fast i' the cream-jug.

Blindly he jumps on the floor,
Crash !—there is no cream-jug more.

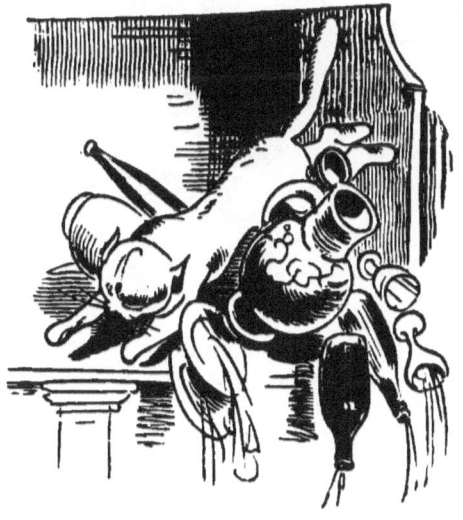

On the side-board now he flies,
And glass and bottles downward shies.

· Terror-struck he rushes nimbly
On the mantle of the " chimbley."

Alas! What mishap do we see?
Down goes Venus d' Medici!

With one good spring, for 'twas not near,
Tom jumps upon the chandelier.

And ring-a-ding, cling cling-a-ling,
Down comes that most expensive thing.

Now master Tom tries to escape,
But is not yet out of the scrape.

Jemima, to reward his caper,
Takes candle, sealing-wax, and paper,

And twists the paper, without fail,
Round master Tommie's hairy tail.

Then takes the sealing-wax and taper,
And to the tail fixes the paper.

At last, incited by her ire,
She the paper sets on fire.

Now may poor master Tommie go,
But feels what the French call "chaud."

CHAPTER VIII.

I'm sure no one needs to be told,
That when the weather's rather cold,
'Tis pleasant to remain in bed
One hour or more; then we feel glad.
Our thoughts move on at wondrous pace.
We take another hour's grace,
And think about what might have been,
If all things could have been foreseen.
At last we're even tired of thinking,
And get up, without any blinking;
To leave our couch we hardly fret,
And now begin our morn toilette.

Very good is cleanliness,
But mankind cannot do less.

For age does our strength impair,

And we even lose our hair.

E

Art supplies the wants of nature,

And enhances a fair creature.
Those things aye for some time last ;
But art does fail, and life goes fast.

Jemima said one morn : " Quite so ;
I'll marry Messrs Plum & Co."

John Plum was in the highest glee,
For he'd propos'd, and was ready.
And when the lovely spring was " cum,"
Jemima became Mistress Plum.

CHAPTER IX.

To Heidelberg, in Germany,
The newly married couple went.

They walked about the lifelong day,
And thus their honeymoon they spent:

"Oh ! darling duckie, see, look here !
These ruins look so very queer."

" It's warm," said Plum ; "and, by the powers,
I'm thirsting for a few good showers."

"To look at ruins is great fun ;
But I prefer the large wine-tun."

"Did you ever?   I must say,"—

" Coachman waits, come, dear, away."

" Quick let's see what's to be seen,
Then back to the hotel, I ween."

Nice ham-chops and " sparrowgrass,"
All things in the world surpass.

"Waiter, Garçon, quickly go,
Bring a bottle of Cliquot."

Runs the waiter without fail,
Moves the coat called swallow-tail.

Lovely looks the golden rain,
In a glass of good champagne.
"Let's drink the health of ma'am Cliquot !"

Jemima reads the paper slow.

"I say, another flask of wine!"
By poor Jemima's watch 'tis nine.

Runs the waiter without fail,
Moves the coat called swallow-tail.

Lovely looks the golden rain,
In a glass of good champagne.

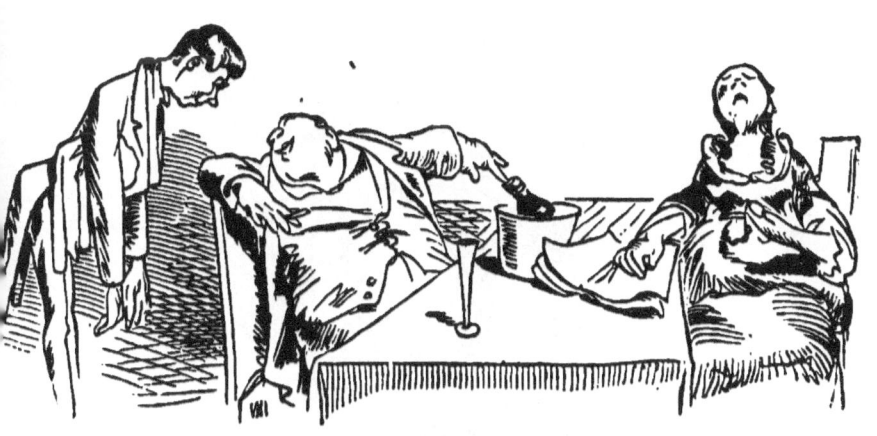

" Another bottle I'll dispatch ! "
It's ten by poor Jemima's watch.

The waiter wants to bolt away,
But Mrs Plum just bids him stay,

And show them, with his light, the way,
For Mister Plum is very gay.

He with his hand puts out the light,

And does not stir that blessed night.

CHAPTER X.

Many ladies, very well off,
Pretty rich, in good society,
Think that time does not move on,
And do not care a fig for piety.

How much more praise deserves Jemima;
She thinketh not like one of those—
No, no! She often walks to church,
And does not mind how far she goes.

And John, with downcast looks demure,
Remains three paces in the rear;
And with a hymn-book in his hand,
Follows his mistress far and near.

But our Jemima studies not
Herself alone.   Oh ! no ! nay ! nay !
She "unco guid" also observes
When others from the right path stray ;
And through instruction oft essays
To mend and to convert their ways.

" What's in your pockets, John ? " quoth she.
" You're fond of sweet things—let me see ? "

"Yes, here it is.   I thought 'twas so.
John ! John !   Think where the wicked go ! "

So piercingly her words did move,
That John swore quickly to improve.

But by good deeds real love is shown,
And not by mouthing words alone.

Jemima knits in leisure time
A jacket fit for a cold clime,
For tempests rage, and do great harm.
She e'en gets ready flannels warm,
In winter-time a regular blessing,
When round the body they are pressing.
She also acts, with great delight,
As nurse to a wounded French "off 'zier,"
Who last year dwelt with many friends
In Germ'ny, not "pour son plaisir."

But what most oft she did bemoan,
Was the poor people's awful lot.
Her doctor said in serious tone,
"You'll take a bath in wine, quite hot."

She took 't.

Oh ! how full of joy
Is now the crowd of "hoi polloi."

Who, to refresh the inner man,
Take a warm drink whene'er they can.

CHAPTER XI.

It is well known, and needs not to be told,
That man and wife in wedlock oft delight,
And that the greatest pleasure on this earth,
Is when a babe first meets the parents' sight ;
Because they are then, without any bother,
A happy father and a happier mother.
But many a time some bickerings arise,
When similar little blessings don't appear.
Poor Mrs Plum discovered this likewise,
And dropped, in lonely sorrow, many a tear.

Near her abode there lived a pious man,
A holy monk, not far from the St Peter,
Praised very much by all the womankind
Of far and near, as learning's chief arbiter.

Now he, alas ! was ill, and kept his bed,
And spoke thus : " Daughter mine," and shook his head.
Then said again : " The case is very serious ;
My dearest, let me speak to you quite plain—
Spiritual means alone cure the mysterious ;
Therefore, I say, walk the steep mountain path,
Follow the holy pilgrims' blessed train,
Which goes towards the church of Saint M'Grath.

In that church stands a cradle quite alone,
Of which the powers were in all ages known.
And whosoever—like Miss Lucy Long,
The lady, far famed now through Christy's song—
That cradle rocks, will, after some delay,
Find out that 'Labor vincit omnia.'

"Alas! alack!   Not many years ago,
There was a maiden pious and devout,
Who never had been taught, e'en till "dato,"
That all things hidden always will come out.
Through childishness, and without any thought,
She rocked the cradle—rocked it, oh! so gently,
That anyone might think 'twould come to nought;
But yet the sequel proved quite differently.

" There came also a wicked pilgrim bold,
Who being curious, touched the cradle merely;
But after a few weeks, so I've been told,
He got his punishment, and that severely.
And so——But, my dear girl, no more to-day;
The bells are ringing, I must my matins say.
May you find consolation on your way.
Farewell!   Go *in pace!*"

CHAPTER XII.

High upon the holy mound,
Church and tavern may be found.
From the vale the pious crowd,
Upon blessed thoughts intent,
Joyful, but with serious mien,
Tread the mountain's steep ascent.
From the bottom of their hearts
Words flow to the labial rims ;
Warm and friendly sounds are breath'd
By the he—and she—pilgrims.

But in front, with dusty shoes,
Warm at heart, and hot at head,
Tired quite oft severely,
The dear brethren take the lead.

Now the sisterhood appears,
Singing sweetly and so well, ah !
Peace dwells in their gentle hearts ;
Their hands hold an " umberella."
Lovely sing the pious fair,
Brother David leads in pray'r.

Yonder, where the sun shines bright,
Jemima walks, sad but serene.
We may say she is quite alone,

For no one near her is seen,
And her excellent cousin Frank,
Is her only associate ;
Who, by all who knew him well,
Was called "holy" Frank of late.—
Like Jane and Johnie in the fair,
Moves that pious pilgrim pair.

Thanks to heaven they have arrived !
Amidst praises rightly won,

And with zeal and calm intent,
Everything that needs be 's done.

They merrily to taverns slink,
And merrily pounce upon drink,
Which brother Will, so long ago,
In the convent, quite solo,
Brewed, with thoughts on beer intent,
Minding not what hops he spent.

And cordially each pious he,
Looks upon each pious she,

At last, after the day's heat,
Th' evening coolness seems so sweet.

In the moonlight's silvery rays,
Jemima walks, glad and serene,
We may say she's quite alone,
For no one near her is seen
But her excellent cousin, Frank,
And his gentle, holy mien.
They homewards go, as from a fair,
That good, pious, pilgrim pair.—

But the noble brotherhood,
And the sisters calm and good,
Stayed behind a little late,
Because they too long had pray'd.
Lovely sing the pious fair,
Brother David leads the pray'r.

See a cab approaches slow,
For the horse has far to go.

He, the driver of the cab,
Reckless and at heart perverse,
Thinks, I won't take off my hat
For anything, except a hearse.—

Upon him each pious he,
And pious she, look'd spitefully.
And the cabby plied the whip,
To give those devotees the slip.

But our David made the whole
Pious brothers' banner's pole,
In the wheels so tightly fit,

That the cab couldn't move a bit.

Each one by his coat and leg,
Tries coachie from his seat to drag.

Dear Miss Nancy with her crutch,
Gave our cabby rather much,
But the lady Lochinvar,
Really drove the thing too far,

For, excited by her zeal,
She her umb'rella used as steel;

Though no damage coachie reaches,
'Cause he wore warm leather breeches!
Look'd on each other, full of glee,

Each pious he, each pious she—
Chaunt afar the maidens fair,
Brother David leads the pray'r.
But the wicked coachman, who

Made 'bout nothing much ado,

Quickly to the court-house went;
There he told his fate so "sair"
To the judge, who then did send
For David, and the maidens fair.

Soon the sentence was pronounc'd,
David got three weeks in quod;
And the he—and she—pilgrims
Had to pay for scot and lot.

Look'd on each other gloomily,
Each pious he, each pious she.

CHAPTER XIII.

The stork, 'tis said, is always full of tricks,
And all the new-born babes out of the water picks.

What we should do if no storks there were
I could not tell, I solemnly declare.

This kindly beast, brought to the Plums last night
Two little babes, a very lovely sight !

Dear cousin Frank look'd full of happiness,
Spoke a few words and said : " I can't do less,
Such little, friendly faces I've seen few !
A double blessing, dear friend, 'tis for you !

Therefore give double praise where it is due !
My dear friend Plum, I must congrat'late you ! "

About twelve o'clock Mister Plum came down,
Looking quite jolly from feet to crown.

To-day salad and fish he'll eat,
Soon at the table takes his seat.

Alas ! a fishbone sticks in Plum's throat;
He coughs till he's blue, but it won't come out.

And coughs so much that whatever he ate,
Flies out of his ears at a very great rate.

Down, down he falls—dies *subito;*
John in seizing the bottle is not slow.

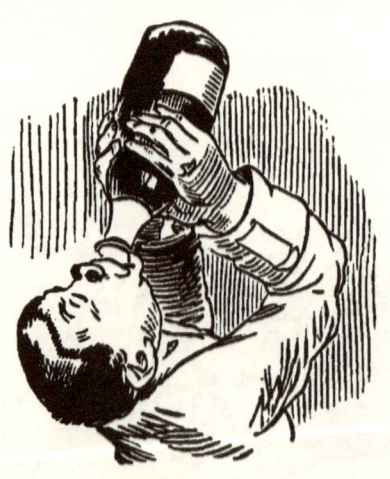

"Oh! oh!" spoke John, "'t surpasses belief;
But 'tis quite sure, man's life is brief!"

CHAPTER XIV.

"Oh, Frank!" Jemima spoke, midst tears,
"Sole friend, who my lone sorrow cheers!"

"Yes!" swore our Frank, with bated breath,
"Sole I was, am, and won't be less!"

"Now, good night; it is nearly ten,
I trust I soon shall come again.

Frank gently down the stairs does tread,
" Hum ! hum ! that Kittie looks not bad ! "

For, as a youth, dear cousin Frank
Played in the kitchen many a prank.

John draws now near, and stealthily,
Observes their close intimacy.

Fired by the demon jealousy,
He lifts the bottle angrily.

Bang! and with all the force he can,
John drives the flask in Frank's brain pan.

Frank's part's played out! oh what a sight
For Mrs Plum!—Down falls the light.

CHAPTER XV.

Alas! by sin is mankind rent!
Jemima, you must soon repent!

She to the cupboard, deeply moved,
Hastens, feeling quite reproved.

"Away! false tresses I have got,
Cosmetics and pomatum-pot!

My heart's support goes i' the fire,
You, stays, which often raised desire !

Away with enticing boots from Paris,
Which once so near, but now so far is !

Frippery, formerly my shame,
Be now purified by flame.

No one minds the world's false scandals,
When he beholds these lovely sandals !

The pretty picture you here see,
Is Jemima as devotee.

CHAPTER XVI.

Quite wisely a sage used to say:
He who has cares drinks cares away!

"No!" shouts Jemima—"'tis quite plain,
I'll never—never—never—never
    never do the like again!

She from afar with fervour prays,
The bottle on the table stays.

She prays devoutly on her knees,
The bottle quietly stands at ease.

One sees not well far from the light,
The bottle moves not out of sight.

Oft people read through idle whims,
The bottle is no book of hymns.

Dang'rous looks your dearest friend,
Jemima, nearer draws the end!

Behold! in holy night-toilette,
Auntie appears, to warn her pet.

In tones unearthly, full of woe
She calls: "Jemima! Mima! oh

Down falls the lamp.   In vain she'd come,
'T sets light to the petroleum.

And shrieking, helpless through dismay,
Devout Jemima coals away.

Smoking remains we here discover,
The rest is of no use whatever.

CHAPTER XVI.

Oh! what a terrible hullabaloo;
'Tis dark, 't thunders, 't lightens too!

H

The tailed infernal mercury,
At th' chimney-pot waits patiently.

Jemima's guardian-angel quick,
Cuts off the tail of grim old Nick.

The latter in a trice turns round,
And throws the angel on the ground.

Alas! alas! what do we see?
The demon gains the victory!

Now the poor soul firm in his hold is,

He takes her down where it ne'er cold is.

Hurrah ! hurrah ! throw her in ! steady !
For holy Frank is here already.

FINALE.

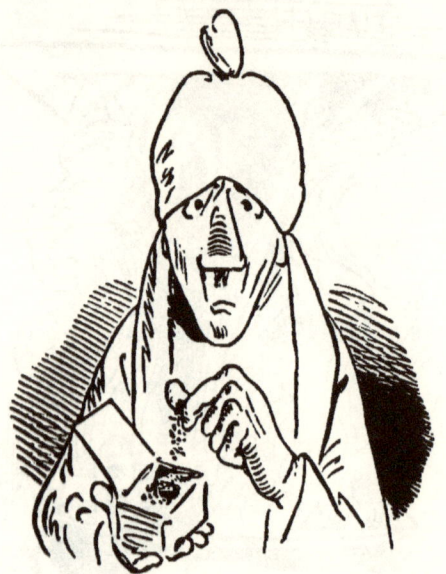

When uncle Jim first heard of this,
He cut a very ugly phiz.

But when he'd vented all his grief,
" I've oft foretold it " gave relief.

"Whene'er good things are left undone,
They're ay called bad by every one.

Now, heaven be praised! my troubles cease,
I'm sure I'm not like one of these!!"

HUGH MILLER'S WORKS.

CHEAP POPULAR EDITIONS,

In crown 8vo, cloth extra, price 5s. each.

Eighteenth Edition.

1. **My Schools and Schoolmasters ; or, The** Story of my Education.

'A story which we have read with pleasure, and shall treasure up in memory for the sake of the manly career narrated, and the glances at old-world manners and distant scenes afforded us by the way.'—*Athenæum.*

Thirty-ninth Thousand.

2. **The Testimony of the Rocks ; or, Geology** in its Bearings on the Two Theologies, Natural and Revealed. *Profusely Illustrated.*

'The most remarkable work of perhaps the most remarkable man of the age. . . . A magnificent epic, and the Principia of Geology.'— *British and Foreign Evangelical Review.*

Ninth Edition.

3. **The Cruise of the Betsey ; or, A Summer** Ramble among the Fossiliferous Deposits of the Hebrides. With Rambles of a Geologist ; or, Ten Thousand Miles over the Fossiliferous Deposits of Scotland.

Fourth Edition.

4. **Sketch-Book of Popular Geology.**

Eleventh Edition.

5. **First Impressions of England and its People.**

'This is precisely the kind of book we should have looked for from the author of the "Old Red Sandstone." Straightforward and earnest in style, rich and varied in matter, these "First Impressions" will add another laurel to the wreath which Mr. Miller has already won for himself.'—*Westminster Review.*

[*Continued on next page.*

HUGH MILLER'S WORKS.

CHEAP POPULAR EDITIONS,

In crown 8vo, cloth extra, price 5s. each.

Ninth Edition.

6. **Scenes and Legends of the North of Scotland**; Or, The Traditional History of Cromarty.

Fourteenth Edition.

7. **The Old Red Sandstone; or, New Walks** in an Old Field. *Profusely Illustrated.*

Fifth Edition.

8. **The Headship of Christ and the Rights** of the Christian People. With Preface by PETER BAYNE, A.M.

Thirteenth Edition.

9. **Footprints of the Creator; or, The Aste-**rolepis of Stromness. With Preface and Notes by Mrs. MILLER, and a Biographical Sketch by Professor AGASSIZ. *Profusely Illustrated.*

Fifth Edition.

10. **Tales and Sketches. Edited, with a Pre-**face, by Mrs. MILLER.

Fourth Edition.

11. **Essays: Historical and Biographical,** Political and Social, Literary and Scientific.

Fourth Edition.

12. **Edinburgh and its Neighbourhood, Geo-**logical and Historical. With the GEOLOGY OF THE BASS ROCK.

Third Edition.

13. **Leading Articles on Various Subjects.** Edited by his Son-in-law, the Rev. JOHN DAVIDSON. With a Characteristic Portrait of the Author, fac-simile from a Photograph by D. O. HILL, R.S.A.

. *Hugh Miller's Works may also be had in complete sets of 13 Volumes elegantly bound in roxburgh style, gilt top, price £3, 18s., or in cloth extra, gold and black printing, new style, gilt top, price £3, 5s.*

POPULAR WORKS BY ASCOTT R. HOPE.

Third Edition, just published, post 8vo, cloth extra, profusely
illustrated, gilt edges, price 5s.,

MY SCHOOLBOY FRIENDS:
A Story of Whitminster Grammar School.

By the Author of 'A Book about Dominies,' 'Stories of School Life,' etc.

'Its fidelity to truth is the charm of the book; but the individuals introduced
are so admirably described, that an excellent moral may be deduced from the
attributes of the well-disposed and the vicious. The volume will be read with
interest by those who have arrived at full age, and with much mental profit by
those who are in their nonage.'—*The Lincoln Mercury.*

'Mr. Hope has already written several excellent stories of schoolboy life; but
this story of "Whitminster Grammar School" excels anything he has yet done.'
—*The North British Mail.*

Fourth Edition, crown 8vo, cloth extra, price 3s. 6d.,

A BOOK ABOUT DOMINIES:
BEING THE REFLECTIONS AND RECOLLECTIONS OF A MEMBER OF THE PROFESSION.

'This is a manly, earnest book. The author describes in a series of essays the
life and work of a schoolmaster; and as he has lived that life and done that work
from deliberate choice, his story is worth hearing.'—*The Spectator.*

Fourth Edition, crown 8vo, cloth extra, price 3s. 6d.,

A BOOK ABOUT BOYS.

By ASCOTT R. HOPE, Author of 'A Book about Dominies,' etc.

'This volume is full of knowledge, both useful and entertaining, in the truest
sense of the words, and it is impossible to put it down without a feeling of per-
sonal kindliness towards the author. If our readers think we have praised too
much and criticised too little, we can only say there is something about the book
which disarms one's critical faculty, and appeals to them to judge for themselves.
We should like to see it in the hands of every parent and schoolmaster in England.'
—*Saturday Review.*

Fourth Edition, just published, in crown 8vo, elegantly bound
and illustrated, gilt edges, price 5s.,

STORIES OF SCHOOL LIFE.
By ASCOTT R. HOPE, AUTHOR OF
'A Book about Boys,' 'A Book about Dominies,' etc. etc.

'A book more thoroughly adapted to boys cannot be found.'—*The Globe.*

[*Continued on next page.*

POPULAR WORKS BY ASCOTT R. HOPE—*continued.*

Second Edition, crown 8vo, cloth extra, price 3s. 6d.,

TEXTS FROM THE TIMES.

By ASCOTT R. HOPE,
Author of 'A Book about Dominies,' 'A Book about Boys,' etc. etc.

'Mr. Hope is a very sensible man, and speaks what is well worth listening to for its good practical common-sense. We wish that some of our novelists would especially study his essay upon the "Novels of the Period." His criticism on the literature of the subject is full of home truths. . . . Let us give, too, a word of praise to his essay "On going to the Theatre." In the main, we thoroughly agree with him. *We,* at all events, shall not be suspected of any design of forbidding cakes and ale; but we fully go with him in his criticism upon the utter stupidity and folly of our modern plays, and the wretched bad acting and the vulgarity of most of our actors and actresses. Mr. Hope's book deserves a place in every lending library both in town and country. It is especially distinguished by its healthy tone, and should be put into the hands of all young people.'—*Westminster Review.*

Third Edition, crown 8vo, elegantly bound, and profusely Illustrated by CHARLES GREEN, price 3s. 6d.,

STORIES ABOUT BOYS.

By ASCOTT R. HOPE,
Author of 'Stories of School Life,' 'My Schoolboy Friends,' etc. etc.

'Boys will find he has prepared a tempting dish, into which they may dip again and again with interest and with profit. The volume is handsomely got up.'—*The Scotsman.*

Just published, crown 8vo, cloth gilt, with numerous Illustrations, price 5s.,

STORIES OF FRENCH SCHOOL LIFE.

By ASCOTT R. HOPE,
Author of 'A Book about Dominies,' 'Stories about Boys,' 'My Schoolboy Friends,' etc.

Just ready, crown 8vo, cloth extra, price 6s.,

MASTER JOHN BULL:
A Holiday Book for Parents and Schoolmasters.
By ASCOTT R. HOPE,
Author of 'A Book about Dominies,' etc. etc.

*' A marvel of cheapness and excellence, even in this age of cheap
literature.—*Observer.

NIMMO'S
LIBRARY EDITION OF STANDARD WORKS,

In large demy 8vo, with Steel Portrait and Vignette, handsomely
bound, roxburgh style, gilt top, price 5s. each.

1. **SHAKESPEARE'S COMPLETE WORKS.** With a
Biographical Sketch by MARY COWDEN CLARKE, a Copious
Glossary, and numerous Illustrations.

₊ This Edition is based on the Text of Johnson, Steevens, and
Reed, which is allowed to be one of the most accurate , and, so far as
regards mechanical correctness, it will contrast favourably with many
high-priced and ambitious editions.

2. **BURNS'S COMPLETE WORKS.** Containing also his
Remarks on Scottish Song, General Correspondence, Letters to
Clarinda, and Correspondence with George Thomson. With
Life and Variorum Notes, and full-page Illustrations by eminent
Artists.

3. **GOLDSMITH'S MISCELLANEOUS WORKS.** Including
'The Vicar of Wakefield,' 'Citizen of the World,' 'Polite Learning,' Poems, Plays, Essays, etc. etc.

4. **LORD BYRON'S POETICAL WORKS.** With Life.
Illustrated with full-page Engravings on Wood by eminent
Artists.

5. **JOSEPHUS:** The Whole Works of Flavius Josephus,
the Jewish Historian. Translated by WILLIAM WHISTON, A.M.
With Life, Portrait, Notes, and Index, etc.

6. **THE ARABIAN NIGHTS' ENTERTAINMENTS.**
Translated from the Arabic. An entirely New and Complete
Edition. With upwards of a Hundred Illustrations on Wood,
drawn by S. J. GROVES.

7. **THE WORKS OF JONATHAN SWIFT, D.D.** Care-
fully selected. Including 'A Tale of a Tub,' 'Gulliver's Travels,'
'Journal to Stella,' 'Captain Creichton,' 'Directions to Servants,'
Essays, Poems, etc. etc. With a Biography of the Author, and
Original and Authentic Notes.

[*Continued on next page.*

'We congratulate the lovers of good literature on having their tastes supplied at such a cheap rate.'—THE CITY PRESS.

NIMMO'S
LIBRARY EDITION OF STANDARD WORKS,
CONTINUED.

In large demy 8vo, with Steel Portrait and Vignette, handsomely bound, roxburgh style, gilt top, price 5s. each.

8. **THE WORKS OF DANIEL DEFOE.** Carefully selected from the most authentic sources. Including 'Robinson Crusoe,' 'Colonel Jack,' 'Memoirs of a Cavalier,' 'Journal of the Plague in London,' 'Duncan Campbell,' 'Complete English Tradesman,' etc. etc. With Life of the Author.

9. **THE WORKS OF TOBIAS SMOLLETT.** Carefully selected from the most authentic sources. Including 'Roderick Random,' 'Peregrine Pickle,' 'Humphry Cliuker,' Plays, Poems. With Life, etc.

10. **THE CANTERBURY TALES AND FAERIE QUEEN:** With other Poems of CHAUCER and SPENSER. Edited for Popular Perusal, with current Illustrative and Explanatory Notes. With Lives of the Authors.

11. **THE WORKS OF THE BRITISH DRAMATISTS.** Carefully selected from the Original Editions. Including the best Plays of BEN JONSON, CHRISTOPHER MARLOWE, BEAUMONT and FLETCHER, PHILIP MASSINGER, etc. etc. With copious Notes, Biographies, and a Historical Introduction.

12. **THE SCOTTISH MINSTREL:** The Songs and Song Writers of Scotland subsequent to Burns. With Biographies, etc. etc. By the Rev. CHARLES ROGERS, LL.D.

13. **MOORE: THE POETICAL WORKS OF THOMAS** MOORE. New Edition, carefully Revised. With Life. Illustrated with full-page Engravings on Wood, by eminent Artists.

14. **FIELDING: THE WRITINGS OF HENRY** FIELDING. Comprising his Celebrated Works of Fiction. With Life, etc.

. *This Series is also kept bound in cloth extra, full gilt side, back, and edges, price 6s. 6d. each; and in quarter green calf, polished back, red cloth sides, price 7s. 6d. each.*

Just ready, in fcap. 8vo, toned paper,

Entirely New Cloth Binding, in various Emblematic Designs worked in Gold and Black, price 3s. 6d.
Entirely New Morocco Bindings, in antique raised, at 6s. 6d., and in extra raised, with high-class Medallion Portraits on side, at 7s. 6d.

NIMMO'S POPULAR EDITION

OF

THE WORKS OF THE POETS.

———o———

In fcap. 8vo, printed on toned paper, elegantly bound in cloth extra, with various emblematic designs worked in gold and black, price 3s. 6d. each; or in morocco antique, price 6s. 6d. each; or morocco extra, raised and with high-class medallion portraits on side, entirely new design, price 7s. 6d. each. Each Volume contains a Memoir, and is illustrated with a Portrait of the Author engraved on Steel, and numerous full-page Illustrations on Wood, from designs by eminent Artists; also beautiful Illuminated Title-page.

〜〜〜〜〜〜〜〜〜

1. LONGFELLOW'S POETICAL WORKS.

2. SCOTT'S POETICAL WORKS.

3. BYRON'S POETICAL WORKS.

4. MOORE'S POETICAL WORKS.

5. WORDSWORTH'S POETICAL WORKS.

6. COWPER'S POETICAL WORKS.

7. MILTON'S POETICAL WORKS.

8. THOMSON'S POETICAL WORKS.

9. GOLDSMITH'S CHOICE WORKS.

10. POPE'S POETICAL WORKS.

[*Continued on next page.*

NIMMO'S POPULAR EDITION OF THE WORKS OF THE POETS,

CONTINUED.

—o—

11. BURNS'S POETICAL WORKS.

12. THE CASQUET OF GEMS.   Choice Selections from the Poets.

13. THE BOOK OF HUMOROUS POETRY.

14. BALLADS : Scottish and English.

15. THE COMPLETE WORKS OF SHAKE-SPEARE.   Two Vols.

16. THE ARABIAN NIGHTS' ENTERTAIN-MENTS.   Two Vols.

17. BUNYAN'S PILGRIM'S PROGRESS AND HOLY WAR.

18. LIVES OF THE BRITISH POETS.

19. THE PROSE WORKS OF ROBERT BURNS.

** This Series of Books, from the very superior manner in which it is produced, is at once the cheapest and handsomest edition of the Poets in the market. The volumes form elegant and appropriate Presents as School Prizes and Gift-Books, either in cloth or morocco.

' They are a marvel of cheapness, some of the volumes extending to as many as 700, and even 900, pages, printed on toned paper in a beautifully clear type. Add to this, that they are profusely illustrated with wood engravings, are elegantly and tastefully bound, and that they are published at 3s. 6d. each, and our recommendation of them is complete.'—*Scotsman.*

www.ingramcontent.com/pod-product-compliance
Lightning Source LLC
Chambersburg PA
CBHW031928060726
47496CB00008BA/2425